Cat's Big Night

by Nancy Krulik
illustrated by Gary Johnson

Simon Spotlight / Nickelodeon

If you purchased this book without a cover you should be
aware that this book is stolen property. It was reported as
"unsold and destroyed" to the publisher and neither the author
nor the publisher has received any payment for
this "stripped book."

Based on the TV series *CatDog*®
created by Peter Hannan as seen on Nickelodeon®

Editorial Consultants: Peter Hannan and Robert Lamoreaux
Additional assistance provided by the CatDog Production Team.

SIMON SPOTLIGHT
An imprint of Simon & Schuster Children's Publishing Division
1230 Avenue of the Americas, New York, New York 10020

Copyright © 1999 Viacom International Inc.
All rights reserved. NICKELODEON, *CatDog*, and all related titles, logos,
and characters are trademarks of Viacom International Inc.

All rights reserved including the right of reproduction in whole or in part in any form.

SIMON SPOTLIGHT and colophon are registered trademarks of Simon & Schuster.

Produced by Bumpy Slide Books
Manufactured in the United States of America

First Edition   10 9 8 7 6 5 4 3 2

ISBN 0-689-83001-7

Library of Congress Catalog Card Number 99-71202

Chapter One

Ding-dong! The doorbell rang at CatDog's house.

"I'll get it!" Dog yelled, as he raced toward the front door.

"No, I'll get it!" Cat shouted as *he* ran for the door.

Unfortunately, neither Cat nor Dog reached the door. All they managed to do was get knotted in the middle like a pretzel.

Winslow popped out from a small door behind the couch. "I'll get it," he said to CatDog. "Must be my fake throw-up from the joke-of-the-month club."

Winslow opened the front door. An

official-looking envelope was lying on the doormat.

Cat began walking toward the door. Dog followed behind. Cat took the letter from Winslow and glanced at the return address.

"Hey! It's from the Museum of Natural History," Cat said. "Maybe they would like me to consult on an Egyptian exhibit," he mused as he tore open the envelope. A card with gold writing on it fell to the floor.

Dog picked it up. "It's an invitation," he said.

Cat grabbed the invitation from Dog and began to read. "You're right. It's an invitation to a fancy party next Friday night. They are opening a new dinosaur exhibit." Cat began to walk regally around the room. "Obviously the museum curators realized that I belong at these society events—especially

one at the museum. With my royal feline background, I'm the perfect—"

Winslow hopped onto Cat's shoulder and looked at the invitation. "It says here your name was chosen at random from the phone book," he said.

"Yes . . . well . . . ahem . . . uh," Cat stammered. "Whatever. I'm invited aren't I? I can't wait to rub elbows with the rich and famous. Now I have so much to do before the party. I'll have to rent a tuxedo, and get myself groomed, and—"

"What are you, nuts?" Winslow interrupted. "You're not going to that party. The invitation is addressed to Cat. Just Cat. And look what it says down here—'no children or dogs allowed.' Well, that leaves you out!"

Cat stopped and looked at his other

half. Dog cocked his head and looked back at Cat. Cat frowned. Cat knew there was no way he could go to that party. Unless . . .

"Well, there is one way . . ." Cat began.

Dog began to shake. The last time Cat had an idea about doing something alone, the brothers had almost been separated by a giant chainsaw. It was not one of Dog's favorite memories.

"Uh, Cat, maybe they'll make an exception and let you bring a dog," Dog suggested nervously.

"No," Cat said. "The invitation is for one cat named Cat. So I'll have to go alone. Or at least it will have to *look* as though I am alone."

Dog stared with curiosity at Cat. He had no idea what his brother was thinking.

"Here's the plan," Cat began. "I'll rent

an extra long tuxedo. One that will cover your head. Then you pretend you're not there. No one will see you, and no one will suspect a thing. I'll look like an ordinary cat. Well, not an ordinary cat exactly, because I am so *extraordinary!*"

Dog smiled. He wasn't sure why this party was so important to his brother. Personally, he'd rather spend an evening chasing squirrels. But if it was what Cat wanted, Dog would help him out. "Okay, Cat. If this will make you happy," he said. "I'll be there for you."

"Good," Cat said. "Now, let's get to that tuxedo rental store."

Just then, Winslow heard a humming sound coming from down the road. "Hey, Dog! Do you hear what I hear?" he asked mischievously.

Dog put his ear to the ground and listened carefully. "Garbage truck!" he shouted. His eyes glazed over. He started chanting over and over. "Must chase garbage truck! Must chase garbage truck! Must chase garbage truck!"

With only that warning, Dog raced after the truck, yanking Cat in the opposite direction of the tuxedo store.

"Hey! What are you doing?!" Cat cried out as his enthusiastic brother dragged him down the bumpy road.

Dog answered, "Garbage, garbage, garbage. Truck, truck, truck!"

Winslow watched as CatDog flew down the street. "I can't wait to see Cat's plan backfire!" he laughed to himself.

Chapter Two

Cat spent all week getting ready for the big event. He had his fur brushed, his whiskers trimmed, and his claws buffed. When the big night finally arrived, he put on his tuxedo.

"Hey! Who turned out the lights?" Dog cried out from under the tux. "I can't see anything."

"Now Dog, we've been through this. You have to be completely covered," Cat explained. "Just follow me. You'll be fine."

"Okay, Cat," Dog agreed.

And with that, Cat headed out for his big night on the town.

Cat was a little nervous as they reached

the museum steps. There were a lot of guards near the entrance. One wrong move by his brother and they would see that a dog was sneaking into the museum. Cat would be tossed out of the party.

But Cat didn't have anything to worry about. Dog was as good as his word. As Cat walked upright, Dog stayed silently hidden under the tuxedo jacket, and Cat breezed right past the guards at the door.

The party was in full swing. Everyone was eating, talking, and dancing to the band playing in the corner. Cat tried to make his way over toward a group of rich high society people, but Dog had already heard the music. Instantly his feet began moving to the beat. Before long, Cat found himself dancing wildly to the music.

"Will you cut that out?" Cat hissed.

"Excuse me?" said a rather large lady cat. She peered over her glasses into Cat's eyes. Since there was no one else around, she thought Cat had been speaking to her.

"I said, uh, um . . . will you look at the spread they've put out," Cat stammered.

"Oh, yes!" the woman replied. "I've already tried one of everything."

As the lady cat walked away, Cat looked to make sure the coast was clear. Then he spoke to Dog again. "You're not supposed to be here, remember?" Cat reminded him.

"Sorry, Cat," Dog apologized. "I'll try and do better."

Cat sighed. He hoped no one else at the party had heard a voice coming from what was supposed to be his rear end.

Cat was hungry. He really needed

something to nibble on. Mmmm. That caviar smelled delicious. Nothing like salty fish eggs! Cat made his way over to the buffet table. But before he could reach over and grab a cracker, a tall, sophisticated cat blocked his path. Cat gulped. It was Randolph. Randolph was the coolest cat in Nearburg! He had never even noticed Cat before. Now here he was, right in front of him!

"You look awfully familiar," Randolph said slowly. "Could we have met in the Alps? I just love those Swiss skis!"

"Swiss cheese?" whispered Dog.

"Shh, Dog!" mumbled Cat, as he tried to look cool.

Randolph shook his head. "No, it was not in the Alps. Perhaps we met sightseeing by the Leaning Tower of Pisa?"

Did someone say "pizza?" Dog thought excitedly.

As Cat and Randolph continued their conversation, Dog sniffed something in the air. He'd know that smell anywhere!

"Tacos! Tacos! Tacos!" Dog whispered excitedly to himself as a waiter passed by with a tray of the tasty Mexican snacks.

Quickly, Dog snuck his arm out from under the tuxedo and grabbed a taco from the tray. He popped the warm cracker, filled with lettuce, tomatoes, cheese, and beans, into his mouth. It was very, very spicy!

Cat was so caught up in his conversation with Randolph that he didn't notice Dog was eating, until he started to feel a burning sensation in the pit of his stomach. He'd felt that way before—usually when Dog had been snacking on pork rinds or chicken gumbo.

"Do you play squash?" Randolph asked Cat.

Yum! Who's got squash? Dog wondered.

Cat opened his mouth to reply to Randolph. But instead he let out a loud, fiery, stinky burp. *"Belch!"*

Randolph stepped back and put his hand over his nose. "Uh, see—I mean smell—you around, old chap," Randolph said, running off as quickly as his feet would carry him.

"Is that your idea of being invisible?" Cat scolded Dog.

"Sorry," Dog apologized. "I was hungry!"

Suddenly there was a loud drum roll. The bandleader took his place by the microphone. "Ladies and gentlemen," he announced, "may I present our special guest for the evening . . . Randolph!"

Randolph took to the stage and

acknowledged the applause. He loved all the attention. "I welcome you all to the museum's new Dinosaur Exhibit," he said. "I personally feel a warm kinship with dinosaurs. After all, they were the bigwigs of their time. And so am I. That reminds me of a story . . ."

Randolph went on and on until someone finally handed him a pair of oversized scissors. He snipped a blue ribbon in two. Then two of the museum's employees opened the curtains that led to the dinosaur exhibit. Cat went to shake Randolph's hand and try to make up for the belching incident.

That's when Dog spotted the largest pile of bones he'd ever seen. Dog raced through the crowd. He completely forgot about his promise to Cat. Dog couldn't think about anything else. He had to have one of those bones, and he had to have it now!

"Bone, bone, bone," Dog chanted over and over to himself.

"Hey!!! What are you doing?" Cat shrieked as Dog dragged him under people's legs, his tuxedo bunching up around his neck. "Cut it out! You're ruining everything!"

But Dog couldn't hear Cat. He was too excited. Quickly, he grabbed a giant bone in his teeth, and ran toward a corner to gnaw on it.

CRASH!

Suddenly, all the partying stopped. The room was completely silent as everyone watched a huge dinosaur skeleton collapse into a heap on the floor.

"We're in big trouble," Cat said. "RUN!"

Now Dog did as he was told. He ran right out of the room and down the cold cement steps of the museum. All the while,

Dog held that giant bone in his mouth.

Cat, of course, was dragged right behind him. For once, Cat kept his mouth shut. He was too angry to say a word!

Chapter Three

CatDog was halfway home before Cat found his tongue again. "How could you do that to me?" Cat demanded. "Aren't I entitled to a night out? Aren't I entitled to a life worthy of my social standing? Why must you ruin everything? *I wish I was never born a CatDog!*"

Dog dropped the giant bone out of his mouth. "I'm sorry," he apologized. "I didn't mean it."

But Cat was still angry. "You ruined my clever plan of disguise. You stole an ancient dinosaur bone. It's probably worth a million dollars. You're going to go to jail for this." Cat gulped as he came to a very important realization. "*We're* going to go to jail for this!" he sobbed.

Dog couldn't bear to see his brother so upset. He hadn't meant to steal anything. He'd just lost his head the minute he'd laid eyes on that big, beautiful bone.

"What can I do, Cat?" pleaded Dog.

"Well, there's only one thing to do," replied Cat.

"Give the bone back?" Dog asked.

Cat nodded.

"Good idea," said Dog. "Thanks, Cat."

Then Dog picked up the bone, and started back toward the museum. Everything would be all right if he just returned the bone.

Suddenly, three dogs popped out from behind a wall of garbage cans and blocked

CatDog's path. Oh, no! It was the Greasers!

"Well, what have we here?" Cliff, the leader of the Greasers, barked.

Dog growled at Cliff.

"Duh, hey looky at dat bone dere," Cliff's buddy Lube pointed out to the others.

Shriek, the smallest of the Greasers, licked her chops hungrily. She smiled flirtatiously at Dog. "That's big enough to be dinner for two," she said.

"Make that dinner for three!" Cliff reminded Shriek. "You, Lube, and me! We're Greasers. We don't share with CatDogs!" Cliff folded his front paw into a tight fist right in front of Dog. "Give up dat bone!" he insisted.

Dog shook his head. He knew the bone belonged in the museum.

"Give up the bone or we squash your

worser half," Cliff insisted, pointing toward Cat.

"Actually, heh, heh, there's no such word as 'worser,'" Cat corrected Cliff nervously.

Cliff glared at Cat.

Cat gulped.

Dog stared at the Greasers. They were already making their way toward Cat. Dog couldn't let them hurt his brother. There was only one thing to do. He dropped the bone at Shriek's feet.

"Take it!" Dog told the Greasers.

"Where'd you get such a big bone?" Shriek demanded, jumping up and down with excitement.

"At the museum," Dog blurted out before he could stop himself. "And there's plenty more like it!"

"Thanks a lot! Beat ya up later!" Cliff shouted as he and the other Greasers ran toward the museum.

Just then, CatDog heard police sirens heading down the street.

"Now you've done it!" Cat shouted. "They're probably looking for that missing bone."

"But I don't have it anymore," Dog laughed. "The Greasers do!"

Cat smiled as the police cars sped past CatDog. Then he heard the Greasers arguing with the police.

"It wasn't us who stole it," Cliff said. "We got it from that no-good thievin' CatDog!"

But the police didn't believe Cliff. "The people at the museum say they didn't see a cat take the bone. They saw a dog.

And you are a dog. And you are holding the bone. Case closed."

The police took the Greasers off to jail.

"I've got to admit, watching those Greasers get busted was a lot of fun. Maybe even more fun than that party," Cat admitted to his brother. "You're not so bad to have around, Dog."

"Thanks, Cat. I was just trying to think about what you would do," replied Dog. "You wouldn't have let them beat me up, would you?"

Cat didn't say anything. He just raised his paw to his brother for a high five.

"CatDog forever!" the brothers shouted happily.

Dog Behind Bars

by Nancy Krulik
illustrated by Gary Johnson

Simon Spotlight / Nickelodeon

Chapter One

Scratch, scratch scratch. Dog listened to the sound of Cat's pen moving back and forth on a piece of paper. Listening to the pen was all Dog could do. He couldn't go anywhere because Cat wouldn't get up from his writing chair. Dog couldn't even talk to Cat, because Cat had given him strict orders never to disturb him while he was writing down very important thoughts.

"Ahhh," Dog sighed quietly.

"Shh!" Cat hissed at his brother. "Can't you see I'm trying to concentrate?"

"How about if you concentrate on playing fetch?" Dog asked. "It's really

beautiful outside. Just go over to the window. You'll see."

"*No*, I will not get up," Cat insisted. "Years from now, historians will find this diary and be fascinated by my thoughts. My ideas will be passed down from generation to generation. You don't want to deny me my place in history, do you?"

Dog shook his head. He couldn't deny his brother anything.

Suddenly a small door slammed opened from behind the lamp. Winslow walked out into the living room. He had something hidden behind his back.

"A little bored, Dog?" Winslow asked.

Dog nodded. "Please whisper, Winslow." "Cat is concentrating on concentrating."

"You want to play or something?" Winslow whispered.

"Shh!" Cat said to them.

Dog shook his head. "I can't. Cat is working."

"Boy, Cat can be a drag," Winslow said. "He never wants to do anything fun like chase squirrels, run after garbage trucks, or dig for bones, does he?"

Dog shook his head sadly. Winslow was right. Dog wished he could do the things ordinary dogs got to do.

Just then, Dog noticed that Winslow was hiding something. "What's behind your back?" Dog asked his little friend.

"Oh, you don't want to know," Winslow replied in a sly voice. "If you see it, you'll want to play with it. And you said you can't play today. So I'll just keep it a secret."

That was all Winslow had to say. Dog *hated* secrets! That was why he didn't like

Cat's diary. Cat never, *ever*, let Dog see what he had written in his diary.

"Please, please, please, Winslow," Dog begged. "Please show me what you have behind your back."

Winslow smiled a sneaky smile. He knew he was causing trouble for Cat. And causing trouble for Cat was Winslow's favorite hobby. "Well, if you insist," he said. He held a bright yellow ball right in front of Dog's face.

Dog's eyes popped wide open. "Ball . . ." said Dog in a hypnotic trance.

"You want to play fetch with it?" Winslow asked Dog.

Dog really wanted to play fetch with that ball. But Cat was still busy writing in his diary. "I can't," Dog told Winslow sadly.

"Okay, then," said Winslow. "If you

really think Cat will mind if you just play one teensy weensy game of fetch." Winslow slowly put the ball behind his back.

Dog couldn't stand it. "Well, maybe one little game wouldn't be too bad," he said.

"That's my pal," Winslow said. He held the ball toward the window.

Dog noticed that the ball had a small string attached to it. He wondered what it was for.

Then Winslow struck a match, lit the string, and threw the ball out the window.

"Okay, Dog," he shouted. "Go fetch the ROCKET BALL!"

Chapter Two

The rocket ball soared through the air at top speed.

"HEEEELLLLLLPPPPP!" yelled Cat as he was suddenly dragged from his desk.

Dog leapt out of the window.

Thump, Thump, Thump.

"Ouch! Ouch! Ouch!" Cat shouted as his head whacked against the window frame.

"See ya later, suckers!" Winslow called after CatDog. Then he went over to the refrigerator, pulled out a big turkey leg, sat down on the couch, and picked up the remote control for the TV. "Now I've got

the whole house to myself," he said with a big grin.

"Fetch! Fetch! Fetch!" Dog repeated over and over as he chased the rocket ball. The ball was flying really fast now. Dog followed the ball everywhere, over mountains, through forests, even up and down the Grand Canyon. When Dog reached the coast of California the rocket ball headed toward the surf.

"NO! NOT THE WATER!" Cat screamed as they flew through the air and landed with a splash in the Pacific Ocean.

But Dog could think of nothing except catching the rocket ball! He dove into the water and started to swim after the ball.

"You know I don't like water!" Cat gurgled.

But Dog couldn't help himself.

As soon as he reached Hawaii, there was a loud explosion. *Kaboom!* A volcano had erupted!

"Ooch! Ouch!" Cat moaned as he was dragged through hot, molten lava.

Dog kept on going. He chased the ball up the steps of the Great Wall of China.

Cat wasn't in such great shape. "Stop, Dog, stop!" cried Cat.

But Dog didn't hear his brother. The rocket ball kept flying and Dog kept running. He sloshed through the swamps of the Australian outback, where the ball flew into a crocodile's mouth. And Dog went right in!

"Hey! Who turned out the lights?"

Cat shouted from deep within the crocodile's mouth.

Luckily, the crocodile was allergic to cats. He coughed and sneezed really hard. The ball flew out of his mouth, with CatDog right behind.

By the time it reached Nearburg, the rocket ball finally fizzled out. Now it was easy for Dog to catch. Dog leapt into the air. He opened his mouth wide—and caught the ball!

Whack! Cat's head slammed right into a brick wall.

"I got it! I got it!" Dog shouted as he dropped the ball on the ground next to Cat.

Cat looked at Dog and rubbed the bump that was growing on his head. "Have you lost your mind, Dog?" he asked angrily.

"One minute I was sitting happily at my desk. And the next minute, I'm . . . I'm . . . where are we anyway?"

Dog looked around. "I'm not sure," he answered. He took a deep breath. "But it *smells* like paradise."

Cat looked around. There was a sign on the brick wall. His eyes widened as he read it. It said *Big City Mega-Dump: The World's Largest Garbage Heap.* Cat was horrified. They were in the big city! And they'd landed right in front of the smelliest, most disgusting garbage heap that Cat had ever seen!

And Cat wasn't the only one who had discovered the gigantic mound of smelly trash.

Dog had already risen to his feet. "Time for a snack!" he shouted. Then he

raced over the wall and began climbing the mountain of garbage, dragging Cat all the way!

"Yum! Yum! Yum!" Dog mumbled, as he chewed on leftover Chinese take-out.

Cat was miserable. "Come on, Dog, that's enough. It's getting dark. You don't want to be stuck here at night, do you?" he asked.

But Dog was having a great time. He'd never seen so much rancid meat before. And he'd worked up quite an appetite running after that ball.

Finally, after Dog had eaten every morsel of food and non-food he could find, he stood at the top of the garbage heap and looked out. The city lights had just come on. "Isn't it beautiful, Cat?" Dog asked his brother.

"Gorgeous," Cat replied sarcastically. "Let's go home."

"Okay," Dog agreed. "Which way is home?"

Cat looked east. He looked west. He looked north and sōuth.

"Let's try this way," suggested Cat.

As they headed west out of the garbage heap, a dog sidled up close beside CatDog.

"Good stuff, huh, dog?" he whispered. "You'll fit in really well here in the city. But do yourself a favor. Lose the cat. We city dogs don't like cats!"

With that, the dog hurried away and disappeared.

Cat gulped. Somehow he had a feeling this was not going to be a great night.

An hour passed and no matter which

way they went, CatDog seemed to end up back in the same place in front of the garbage heap.

"I'll be able to find our way home in the daylight," Cat told his brother. He sighed. "But we're stuck here until morning."

Chapter Three

"Now see what you've done!" Cat shouted at his brother. "I'm going to get killed out here. City dogs don't play games."

Dog looked sheepishly at the ground. He hadn't meant to get Cat in danger. He'd just wanted to have a little fun.

"Don't worry, Cat. I'll protect you," Dog said.

"*You* won't be able to save me from tough city dogs," Cat said.

Dog looked around the garbage heap. He saw a bent bicycle, sandwich wrappers, coffee cups, and empty boxes. Finally, his eyes rested on a big toilet plunger. "That's

it!" he exclaimed. "I'll hide you with that."

Cat looked curiously at Dog. "You're going to hide me with a plunger?" he asked. "How are you going to do that?"

"Like this," Dog said. He picked up the plunger and stuck it on Cat's face. "Now no one can see you, and the wooden stick looks like a tail," he explained.

"Turr-rrific! I'll never forget this!" mumbled Cat angrily.

"Don't mention it!" replied Dog.

>● >● >●

Dog took a few more bites of leftovers, but he really wasn't hungry anymore. He just wanted to find a safe spot nearby to sleep, before he and Cat headed home in the morning. Dog walked around the mountain of garbage. Cat followed behind,

with the plunger on his head, in total darkness.

"Where are we going, Dog?" Cat mumbled. "I can't see a thing!"

"Trust me," replied Dog. "I've got it all under control."

Dog soon found himself in a dark secluded area. In the distance, he could hear howling. It was music to Dog's ears and he *loved* music!

Finally, he reached the source of the sounds. A whole group of dogs were howling at the moon. Dog was so excited! The next thing Cat knew was that his brother was howling—off key—and at the top of his lungs.

Cat wanted to rip that plunger off his head and stick it over Dog's mouth. This was the kind of music that made the fur on

the back of Cat's neck stand up. But Cat knew that if those city dogs found out there was a cat nearby, CatDog would be in major trouble!

Finally, the howling dogs took a break. Dog walked over to a big red fire hydrant, and hung out with the other dogs. Cat breathed a sigh of relief. Maybe now he and Dog could leave.

No such luck.

"Garbage, howling, and fire hydrants. There's nothing like a dog's life is there, buddy?" one of the singing dogs asked Dog.

"You said it!" replied Dog, grinning. He fit right in. He felt very lucky to be a dog. Strangely enough, he didn't miss being a CatDog at all. Just then a beautiful stray mutt walked over to Dog. She batted her long, curly eyelashes and smiled.

"We're all going to have a midnight swim at the lake," she said. "You want to come with us, new guy?"

Dog knew that Cat hated water. He knew he should probably say no, for Cat's sake. But Dog couldn't help himself. He stared into the eyes of the beautiful mutt and smiled helplessly.

"Would I ever!" Dog replied dreamily.

Suddenly, Dog heard a loud siren. It came from a big white truck which was racing down the street.

"Run!" a dog yelled. "It's the dogcatcher!"

Chapter Four

Before Dog knew what was happening, someone grabbed him and threw him into the white truck. It was dark inside, and there seemed to be hundreds of dogs in the truck. They were all howling, barking, and yipping.

Dog was really scared. He didn't know what was going to happen next. He was glad his brother was with him. And Cat was smart. He'd know how to get out of this mess.

But just as Dog was about to ask Cat's advice, he looked over and saw the plunger sticking up where Cat's face usually was.

Oh, no! Dog couldn't ask Cat what to do. Cat wasn't even supposed to be there! Now Dog was sorry he had ever wished to be just an ordinary dog.

Finally, the truck stopped. The dogcatcher got out and opened the back door. The dogs piled out of the truck and were led into a big room. Rancid Rabbit, the dogcatcher, slammed the door shut.

"Hey, where are we?" Dog asked Rancid Rabbit through the metal bars.

"The pound," Rancid replied. "All dogs go to the pound."

"How come?" asked Dog.

"Because I said so," Rancid said simply and walked away.

Dog sadly sat in a corner of the cell. This was horrible. He couldn't stand it any more. He had to talk to Cat! Dog looked

around. The other dogs seemed to be too busy trying to get out of the cell to pay any attention to him. This was the perfect time to chat with Cat.

"Cat, listen, we're stuck in the dog pound. How can we get out of here?" Dog whispered in the direction of the plunger.

Before Cat could reply, a poodle pointed to Dog and began shouting. "This guy's gone nuts!" he yelled. "He's talking to his tail!"

All the other dogs ran to the other side of the cell. No one wanted to be near a crazy dog.

"Did you say *dog* pound?" whispered Cat from under the rubber plunger.

"Uh huh," Dog answered.

"Okay, I think I can get us out of here," Cat told Dog. "Take this plunger

off my head and put it on yours."

"But Cat, the dogs will—" Dog began.

"Just do it!" Cat interrupted him.

Dog did as he was told. He yanked the plunger off of Cat's face. *Boing!!!* Cat's head popped up like a jack-in-the-box. Dog plopped the plunger on his own head.

Suddenly, all the dogs in the room started barking ferociously at Cat. Cat quickly ran to the top of the bars and held on—tight!

Rancid Rabbit raced over toward the cell. "What's going on in there?" he demanded.

Cat peeked down between the bars at Rancid Rabbit. "I believe there's been a mistake here!" he shouted over the barking dogs. "This is a dog pound. I am a cat. I demand to be set free."

Rancid looked confused. "You're not supposed to be in there," he said.

"Tell me about it," Cat replied. "Now if you would just open this door and let me out, please."

The dogcatcher took the key from his pocket and opened the door. Cat walked proudly out of the cell. The other dogs rushed for the door, but Rancid slammed it shut.

Cat turned to the other dogs. "Yeah, see you later," he said with a smirk. "If I get a chance, I'll bake you a cake with a file in it."

Chapter Five

The morning sun was rising as CatDog left the pound and stepped onto the city streets.

They went back to the garbage dump. Cat located the old bicycle he'd seen the night before. Then he yanked the plunger off Dog's head.

"You pedal and I'll steer," said Cat. "We'll be home in no time!"

"Boy, Cat, that was great," Dog said as he pumped his paws up and down on the pedals. "You saved us! I really owe you one!"

"Yes, you do!" Cat said.

"I'm glad we're a CatDog," continued Dog. "Otherwise we'd still be behind bars."

"You mean *you'd* still be behind bars," Cat corrected him.

"We sure make a good team!" Dog said with a smile.

When CatDog finally reached their house, Cat led the way upstairs. He sat down at his desk, pulled out his diary, and got back to writing down his very important thoughts.

Dog sat on the floor beside him. He was careful not to move or speak.

Finally, Cat spoke. "Dog, do you want to see what I've written in my diary today?

Dog bounced up and down with excitement. Wow! Cat was finally letting him read his diary.

Dog picked up his head and peered into the small book. He looked at the page in front of him. It read,

Dear Diary,
Today was a day I'll never forget.
I almost drowned, I landed in the
Mount Everest of garbage dumps,
and even served time in the pound!

Dog looked up and smiled. "Ah . . . that *was* fun!" he exclaimed.

"No, Dog . . . that was PAIN!" Cat replied. Then he settled down for a long overdue nap.

The End

Flip this book over and read my story!

Flip this book over and read about me,
read about me, read about me!

The End